quid pro beau

Kat Baxter

Quid Pro Beau

Kat Baxter

Edited by: Emily Beierle-McKaskle

Copyeditor: BookReadingJenn

Book cover: Cormar Covers

Cover image: CJC Photography

Cover model: David Wills

Formatted with Vellum

quid pro beau

BEAU

I've never been anyone's first choice. Not growing up, not in the military, and definitely not since I got back. Hell, I had to move to someone else's home town because I didn't belong anywhere. Then I meet Daisy. The first woman who makes me feel like I could be enough. But Daisy is off limits. She's my buddy's little sister, and let's not forget that she's pregnant with another man's baby.

Daisy

I came home, tail between my legs, pregnant and heartbroken, ready to start over. The last thing I need is to spend all my time with a charming ex-Ranger. But one quid pro quo later and I'm fostering a dog and Beau is my new birthing coach. Next thing I know it's Beau who's there for midnight cravings and breathing exercises. Beau is the one helping me research the best car seats and rubbing my feet. Now we're sharing a house, a leash and more heat than I know what to do with. But handsome smooth talkers like Beau never stick around for long. I shouldn't want him. I can't trust him. But, oh how I wish I could.

chapter one

DAISY

I've always lived a rather quiet life. You might even say a boring one. I grew up in a normal family: one older brother, a dad who was a high school math teacher, and a mom who was an assistant librarian. We lived in a pretty standard two-story house on a quiet-ish street in a suburb of Houston.

I've never wanted to stand out in a crowd. I don't particularly like drama. I guess you could say I'm shy. Perfectly content to support my loved ones from the shadows. It's why my best friend Temple and I work so well together. She's all gregariousness and sunshine, and I'm just quiet. Contemplative.

But now Temple is married to my brother, Flynn. It happened a couple of years ago and was supposed to be a marriage in name only for her inheritance. The last few weeks though, things have changed dramatically between them. Turns out they're in love. Like in love, in love.

I'm beyond happy for them. Now Temple is my actual sister, and I couldn't have asked for a better wife for Flynn. They're perfect for each other, and I can't believe I never noticed that before.

Still, I can't help feeling a bit like they left me behind. Yes, I know how petty that sounds! Please don't get me wrong. I am so happy for them! I'd never tell either of them, but I'm feeling more alone than I ever have in my life.

My parents retired to Florida a few years ago, and they are loving their life, getting to fish and play on the beach whenever they want. I know my mom would be here in a heartbeat if I called her. But I should be able to handle this situation. I mean I made my bed, so to speak, so now I must lie in it.

Isn't that the old saying?

So yeah, I'm a drama-free llama, except for the fact that my life lately has been nonstop drama. I'm really ready for things to slow down, but I know they won't. At least not anytime soon.

I'm getting a little ahead of myself here.

A week ago I showed up on my big brother's doorstep, here in this small town of Saddle Creek, where he'd moved. I'd taken one look at him and burst into tears.

Flynn pulls me into a tight bearhug. "Hey Angel," he calls behind him. "Put some clothes on, we have company."

"Who is it?" Temple yells.

My brother settles me on the couch with a bottle of water.

"It's Daisy," he says.

"Daisy!" she squeals.

That makes me smile, even if it is a watery one.

"I have missed you so much," Temple says as she rushes into the living room. She practically tackles me on the couch.

"I'm so sorry I missed your grandmother's funeral. I wanted to be here. I tried." I sniff.

My best friend's brow furrows. "Hey, do not think another moment about it. You're here now; that's what matters."

I glance between my best friend and my brother. I can see the difference between them. I know they're married for real now because I've texted back and forth with each of them separately, then all three of us together in a video chat. "I can't believe y'all are all in love and married."

"We are," Flynn says. He smiles widely, then reaches over to squeeze Temple's knee.

"You both deserve to be happy," I tell them.

I take a sobering breath, then just rip off the proverbial bandage. "I have news," I say, with another sniff of my nose. "I'm pregnant."

And those words break the damn of tears. Sobs rattle through me and Flynn jumps up to grab a roll of toilet paper.

"I'm sorry, I don't have any tissues."

I gratefully take the roll and blow my nose.

"Sweetie, why is that sad?" Temple asks. "Or is it just hormones? Babies are not always timely, but they're always a blessing."

"It's not the baby. It's that I have to do it all alone," I say. Then I exhale slowly. "Turns out my perfect British boyfriend wasn't so perfect at all. He'd been separated from his wife, divorce papers in hand. At least that's what he told me."

My brother paces the small length of the living room. Piglet, Temple's dog paces with him. It's ridiculously cute, but I can't even find it in me to laugh at the moment. "Do you want me to kill him?" Flynn asks. "I can make it look like an accident."

"No," I say with a shake of my head. "He's not worth it. He went back to his wife. She's pregnant too, it seems. He gave me a lump sum amount of cash for a trust fund for the baby, signed off on his parental rights, and paid for me to come back home."

"You don't worry about a thing," Temple says, wrapping her arm around my shoulders. "We've got you."

And that's how I ended up living in this charming new town. The downtown square is full of people today. Not quite a full-blown festival, but there are still booths and other things set up near the shops and eateries in town. Dog Days, is what they're calling it, and the proceeds raised today go to the non-profit Great Dane's

Dog Sanctuary. Since Flynn works there with his former Ranger buddies, I know it's a great organization.

I haven't been out there yet, but I keep meaning to go. I was assured—or rather Flynn was assured—that they would find a job for me if I needed one. I still have leftover funds that Timothy gave me, and frankly, I have no qualms about living off of them for the time being. What an asshat!

It seems the entire town has come out in support today and there are people everywhere. Couples with babies in strollers and toddlers riding high on daddies' shoulders fill the streets. Some of them have dogs on leashes. They're buying dog themed everything. Of course there are some treats specifically for dogs, but most are for humans.

Like the gourmet ice cream sandwich I had that was shaped like a bone. It was delicious, so I don't much care what it looked like. I got tired of introducing myself about twenty minutes ago. Don't get me wrong, everyone is genuinely friendly, and that's amazing, and I truly feel welcomed. But I needed to step away.

So I'm currently across the street in the beau-

tiful green park that surrounds the old county courthouse. It's one of those massive, three-story limestone courthouses you see on postcards. It's surrounded by live oaks with trunks as big around as whiskey barrels and limbs that dip gracefully toward the ground and practically beg to be climbed by children. There's a gazebo in the center of the park where someone is picking away on an acoustic guitar. There are giggling children, laughing couples, and even a couple of old codgers playing dominos.

Everything is so perfect, so picturesque, so mother-fricking charming, I half wonder if I've stumbled into a simulation courtesy of the Matrix. One of those first ones that Agent Smith said they made too perfect and the human brain just automatically rejected.

Everything is so perfect.

Except me.

Here I am, sitting in the shade of one of trees, quietly hating everyone else's effortless joy and trying not to burst into tears.

Normally, I enjoy being alone. I relish my solitude. But not now. Now, when I'm by myself, my brain is on a hamster wheel of all the mistakes I made while living in London.

Like how I ended up pregnant by a man who conveniently forgot to mention he had a wife and two kids, with another on the way. I pluck up a piece of grass and shred it with my nails, so exhausted from the mental beatdown I give myself on a daily basis.

The truth is, yes, I feel like a complete moron for believing all of Timothy's lies. I fell fast and hard for his pretty face and even prettier words. I'm not sad I'm pregnant. It's not a perfect situation considering I'm single and likely always will be. But I at least had the common sense to get knocked up by a rich guy who basically set up a fund that will allow my kiddo to want for virtually nothing.

Okay, that had nothing to do with common sense. Just luck. Maybe. I don't know.

Out of the corner of my eye, I see movement. Then there's a big dog with mismatched eyes—one blue and one brown—staring at me. He has no leash trailing behind him as he walks up and lays down at my side.

"Well, hello there," I say to him.

His eyes watch me as I lean forward and give him my hand to sniff. "I'm Daisy. Who might you be?" With a canine huff, he plops his head on my legs.

"You're just the sweetest, aren't you? How did you know I needed a friend today?" I scratch him between the ears, and he makes one of those satisfied doggy noises.

"I don't know about you, but I've made a real mess of my life lately. I had this plan, ya know? I was supposed to be in England, finishing my certification, doing something meaningful with music therapy. Helping people heal. Instead, I'm back in Texas, freshly heartbroken, pregnant, and relatively homeless."

The dog's eyebrows quirk as I speak.

"And now my big brother and my best friend are all in love. They're so adorable. Somehow I've become the third wheel in my own dumb life."

I scratch the pup between his furry ears. His tongue lolls to the side. "You're just the bestest boy," I whisper. "Wanna come home with me?"

"Yes," says a low, amused voice behind me. "I'd very much like to go home with you."

I startle, my heart skydiving straight into my belly. The dog doesn't move. I turn my head to see the origin of the voice and find... gah... I don't even know how to describe him.

Tall, dark and handsome doesn't do this man justice. Not only that, he's not exactly dark. I'd guess that the hair hiding beneath his backwards ballcap—why is that so damn sexy?—is a dark or dirty blond. Golden-brown eyes meet mine and I swear something inside me tightens. My uterus? My heart? Nope, we do not care about tightening body parts.

Do not look directly at the pretty man. Look away. Focus on the dog.

"I wasn't talking to you," I say, managing more sass than I actually feel.

The man crouches beside me, though admittedly not too close. "I realize. But listen, I'd do whatever it takes to get you to call me your bestest boy."

That makes me laugh. Out loud. Then the laugh keeps going.

The beautiful man smiles, laugh lines flare from the sides of his eyes and one dimple pops in his left cheek. "I'm Beau, by the way. Nice to meet you, Daisy."

"You're a shameless flirt, aren't you?" I ask. Then I think better of it and shake my head. "Don't answer that. Is this your dog?"

"Not officially. He's from Great Dane's but

he got away from me." He holds up a blue leash. He pets the dog's belly. "He doesn't like people. Came to the sanctuary skittish as hell. Spooks at everything. I brought him today to see if I could socialize him more."

"He came right over to me, plopped himself down in my lap."

Those whiskey brown eyes meet mine, then boldly rake down my form. "I can't blame him. Your lap looks very comfortable."

If I weren't pregnant by another man's baby, maybe I would take the bait and say something flirtatious back. But I am done with men. Especially those of the I'm-too-hot-for-my-own-good type. I give the pup another scratch, then stand.

"Well, I should be on my way. Have a nice day." Then I turn and walk away. By some miracle, I don't turn around to look at the man or the dog.

chapter two

BEAU

I jump down from my truck and grab Mouse's leash to bring him with me. I never thought I'd be that guy that brings his dog everywhere, but here we are. In part, it's because Mouse is still skittish. For being a big dog—half Husky, half German Shepherd—he's just nervous. My guess, he was mistreated somewhere before he found his way to Great Dane's.

He and I have that in common, I suppose. Mysterious, likely abusive pasts with residual trauma. His has made him not trust many people. I suppose mine has done the same, but I also have the visible evidence of my past. Tattoos cover some of the scars, but not my most recent ones.

Saddle Creek's VFW hall is on the new side, I'm told. It's not super fancy, but it's clean and large, which makes it very serviceable. It's made for a great meeting place for me and the guys.

The guys being ex Rangers like me. We all served together at one time or another. Now we're all retired and living in this small Texas town. Dane is from here, and it's his land that houses the dog sanctuary. Jack came here because he didn't have anywhere else to go and then met and fell in love with his wife, Lucy.

The rest of the guys—Evan, Cruz AKA Romeo, and Liam—all moved here from their respective hometowns. Me? I've never belonged anywhere except the Army, so I figured I'd give Saddle Creek a try and see how the dog sanctuary life worked for me. Frankly, I thought I'd be here a week, maybe two before I moved on. But it's been a little over two months now and I've even rented a house. Turns out, working with my Ranger brothers and dogs is a perfect fucking fit.

Shortly after arriving here, I took an online

training course to get certified in dog obedience. I've designed an agility course for them, and sooner or later all of the dogs will find their way to me. But Mouse, he's mine. He took to me immediately. Just like earlier today when he found Daisy.

Can't say I blame him when it comes to her. She's the prettiest thing I've ever seen. A mop of long blonde hair and the smile of an angel. I'd seen her sitting there against that tree, Mouse, somehow laying across her lap like he belonged there. That image had scratched at something inside me. I'm not even sure what it was. But it had given me enough pause that I was able to hear her speak to my pup before I approached her.

As I step inside the VFW, I'm hit with the scent of freshly brewed coffee. My nose twitches at the smell. All these years and I still am not a fan of the beverage. Kind of sucks because chances are it could have helped me with my ADHD. Instead, I rely on copious amounts of exercise to manage my excess of energy and lack of dopamine.

I lead Mouse over to where my buddies are already sitting. Romeo is carving something out of wood, which is an excellent way of channeling his expert knife skills.

Dane and Jack are talking about the plans their wives made without consulting them. Liam is reading on his e-reader, and Evan and Flynn are in a quiet discussion.

"Sorry I'm late," I tell them as I pull out a chair and sit next to Liam. I don't even bother trying to see what he's reading. Unless he's set his reader to the special dyslexic font, I won't be able to tell. "Mouse got away from me downtown."

Flynn answers his phone and stands but doesn't quite make it away from our table before he's agreeing to whomever is on the phone, then hanging up.

Liam sets down his e-reader.

"Everything okay?" Evan asks. He's always been the sensitive one in our group. Of course he's also the youngest, so he hasn't lived quite long enough to be jaded like I am. But also, he comes from a close-knit family.

Flynn braces his hands on the table. "I need a favor."

Romeo doesn't look up from his whittling. "Is it illegal?"

"If it is, I'm in," I say. Of course I'm only

joking. I might have had a messed-up childhood and adolescence, but I don't break the law.

Flynn rolls his eyes at me. "No, it's not illegal. It's family." He blows out a breath "Temple and I need to go to Houston to deal with some issues with her grandmother's estate." His jaw tightens, then he adds, "We're hoping we'll only be gone about a week."

"If this is about that thing your wife calls a dog, I'm out," Dane says.

"Piglet *IS* a dog, but no, he will be going with us," Flynn says.

"Isn't he like surgically attached to your body at this point?" Liam asks.

"Y'all are fucking hilarious. Anyone want to know about my actual favor?"

"Keep your panties on," Romeo says. He sets down his whittling. Cruz Romero is the oldest in our group and often the voice of reason. That said, he's the first one to give you shit when you screw up, and he never misses an opportunity to flirt with women. Thus the reason we call him Romeo. All except Flynn who's always just called him Cruz.

"We're all ears." Romeo motions with his hands for Flynn to continue.

Flynn nods in thanks. "My sister showed up, unexpectedly, about a week ago. She's been crashing on our couch."

"In your tiny ass cabin?" Liam asks. "That's close quarters for three grown adults."

"Not to mention newlyweds who can't keep their hands off each other," Evan says.

"In any case, with Temple and I leaving, Daisy is going to be all alone."

Wait, did he say Daisy? Surely it's not the same woman I met earlier today. Life is not that fucking cruel. Oh wait, for me, it definitely is.

"I told you if she needs a job, we can find something for her out at the sanctuary," Dane says. "Or you know I have a passel of siblings, and surely someone can help find her a job."

"I really appreciate it," Flynn says. "For now, I think she's just trying to get back on her feet. She's pregnant. By a total piece of shit. I won't go into the gory details, but she needs a new beginning, and Saddle Creek is it."

"I take it the piece of shit isn't in the picture?" Romeo asks.

"Fuck no. And he better not show his face on this side of the pond anytime soon."

Ah, so he's a British piece of shit. Or at least lives over there.

"Daisy is strong and she'll make it through this, but I just hate to leave her when she just got here. New to town and all," Flynn says.

"Don't worry about her," Jack says. "We can introduce her to Lucy and Shelby, and she'll be well on her way to making friends with every decent woman in Bluebonnet County."

Flynn nods. "Appreciate it."

"You worried the sperm donor is going to make an appearance?" I ask.

"No, not really. But then again, I don't know the asshole. So who knows."

"We've got you, Flynn," Romeo says. "Will she be staying at your cabin while you're gone?"

"Yes."

"I'll watch over her."

"I thought your new place was ready?" I ask Romeo.

"It is, but I can stay in my cabin while Flynn is gone just to keep an eye on things."

Flynn reaches over and squeezes Cruz's shoulder. "Thank you, brother. I truly appreciate it."

"We'll all watch out for her," I add.

Flynn's head turns to look at me—his movement so precise it's almost in slow motion. "Do I need to tell you or anyone else that my little sister is off limits?"

I hold my hands up in innocence. If my Daisy is the same as Flynn's Daisy, she is off limits. Hell, most women should be for me. I'm not a family kind of guy. I'm the fun for a night guy. Or a fling for the weekend guy. Definitely not the one you want next to you while you're raising your baby.

"I hear you loud and clear," I tell him.

"Good."

"Okay, now that all of that is settled, can we get to the business we need to cover?" Liam asks.

But my mind is too busy thinking of Daisy and how I can't fucking touch her.

chapter three

BEAU

It's been three days.

I'm not normally one to mark time like this, but the truth is, the day I met Daisy feels monumental in some capacity. So my brain has been keeping track. Three days since I met her. Three days since her brother—one of my best friends—told me she was off-limits.

Of course she's off-limits. For so many reasons. Her being Flynn's sister is just one of them. How about the fact that she's pregnant. I don't have anything against babies or single mothers. But I am not dad material. So there's no reason for me to even pretend otherwise. Even without her impending motherhood, Daisy is a wife-her-up kind of woman.

I don't have those skills either.

When you've never been a part of a functional family, you can't ever cross that line. I've never seen a husband and wife in action. Okay, not like that kind of action. I just mean, I don't know how to be a husband. Watching my buddies Dane and Jack do it just doesn't count. They found their other halves.

Pretty sure men like me don't get those. Hell, as scarred as I am on the outside and as fucked up as I am on the inside, I'm pretty sure I don't have enough of me left to make up half of a couple.

So yeah, Daisy is a no-fly zone. A suicide mission you don't expect to come home from. Even knowing all that, I'm drawn to her in ways even I don't understand.

I tell myself I'm just being a good friend to Flynn. Checking in to make sure his sister is okay in this brand new town.

But that's all a lie.

Yesterday I managed to just drive by the row of small cabins. Twice. Before I made my way back home.

Today I've parked my truck down the street and snapped on Mouse's leash.

What are you doing, Stevens?

I don't know. I only know that I can't stop myself from doing it.

I've barely made it half of a mile from my truck when my phone rings.

I tap my earbud to answer.

"What are you doing, asshole?"

"Good morning to you to, Romeo. Why am I an asshole?"

"Where are you?"

That question gives me pause.

"Are you reconning me?" I ask.

Romeo chuckles. "Nope. I can see you just from looking out my front window, which is what I was doing."

"Who were you looking for?"

"Irrelevant. The point is, what the hell are you doing over here on this side of town?"

"Saddle Creek is a small town, Romeo. It's hardly fair to say it has sides."

Silence comes from the other end of the phone.

I sigh. "I'm walking Mouse."

"Ten miles from your house."

"It's not ten miles." More like seven, but what the fuck ever!

"You're playing with fire, brother."

"By walking my dog? Hardly." Am I being deliberately obtuse? Yes, of course I am. Does Romeo know what I'm doing? Also, yes. Still, I'm not ready to admit to my—whatever *this* is, because it is most definitely *not* an obsession.

"So you drove your truck to this side—over here, away from your house—to walk your dog?"

"You know how skittish Mouse is. There are some corgis in my neighborhood and their barking at the fence always makes Mouse nervous," I say.

"Corgis?"

"Yes. Two of them. They're a menace."

"They're smaller than my feet."

"Only because you're a big motherfucker." I exhale. "Was there a point to this phone call?"

"Just a reminder that Flynn was pretty clear on Daisy being off-limits," Romeo says.

"I'm just walking my dog."

"Dude, I saw the way you looked at her when Flynn brought her out to the sanctuary," Romeo says.

I look up then and see the sun glint off of

some golden curls. My heart thunders in my chest. For fuck's sake, I've become a damned cliche. But that is obviously *her* walking towards me.

"I'm hanging up on you," I tell my buddy.

He just laughs.

Daisy's thick curves are outlined by a bright pink sports bra that is barely containing her magnificent tits. Her hips and thighs are encased in some sort of black, skintight fabric clearly handed down from the gods. It clings and molds, accenting the flare of her wide hips and the shapely curves of her thighs. Goddammit if I'm not getting a fucking hard on just watching her walk towards me.

I stop my progress on the sidewalk as she draws closer. Recognition lights her features.

"Beau? Right?" she says in that sweet voice of hers.

"Yeah," I say, conversation genius that I am.

Her cheeks are flushed pink, and that color continues down her throat onto the pale, freckled skin above her distracting cleavage. She's the prettiest woman I've ever seen in real life. Probably the prettiest woman in the world.

Mouse immediately walks over to her and

presses his leg against her body. When he does that on me, he hits my thigh. But on Daisy since she's not tall and he is, he hits her right in the belly. She scratches his chin, and he looks up at her, completely smitten.

I get it buddy, I really do. I don't understand it, but I get it.

Maybe it's her pheromones.

What am I even saying?

Mouse shifts his body back to me.

"It's almost too hot out here to walk," Daisy says. She holds up the t-shirt she was wearing, now discarded across her shoulder. "Normally I wouldn't just walk around town like this, but it is too hot out here. Not sure if it's the hormones or what."

I want to tell her that she should always dress like that. Or wear even less. Any of that would work well for me. But seriously, it's like my brain has left the building.

"You look perfect," I say, then glance away, clearing my throat. "That is to say, I hear you about the heat. I normally end up taking mine off too."

Which is completely a lie. I would never take my shirt off out here in the open. And bare all of my scars for the entire town to see? No thank you. Still, I just said those words to her. They seem to give her some comfort because she smiles at me.

I'm not sure which of us has moved closer to the other, but we are standing pretty close now. I can see the green ring around the blue of her eyes.

Then she yelps and falls forward against my chest.

Instinctively I grab her by the hips to stabilize her. That's when I look down to see that Mouse has effectively wrapped us together with his leash.

Daisy notices too and laughs.

The sound is pure magic and feels like warm sunshine spreading through my body.

Her hands fist in my shirt. My hands fit to her soft curves like they were meant to hold them. Our bodies press together in one surprisingly intimate knot. And for a second—just one stupid second—we both freeze.

Her breath brushes against my throat, quick and sweet, and her eyes lock onto mine.

Mouse, of course, sits on his ass like this moment is his greatest achievement.

With her body pressed against mine, I can

feel the weight of her baby bump. I think that's what they're called. I don't know.

And all I can think of is that she's growing a person in there, another human being. She's just growing it.

I don't think I've ever, in my life, been more in awe of another person than I am of her. Even though I know women do this sort of thing all the time. But other women aren't pressed against me, smelling sweet and looking heartbreakingly beautiful with the wisps of curls framing her face.

The truth is simple: even though I don't quite understand it, I just know other women aren't Daisy.

"I don't know," I say. "I'm probably not even going to ask this the right way. But, you know, I've never had a sister or mom or whatever, so I don't know, but like, when does the baby come?"

She smiles. "You mean how far along am I, or when is the due date? Those are generally the way people ask."

"Right." I shrug. "Yeah, so when is that? Sorry if that's too personal of a question. Your brother had mentioned that you were pregnant and—"

"You can feel my pregnant belly, all sweat slicked pressed against you," she says.

Fuck, why does that sound so delicious and filthy when she describes it like that?

"I'm about eighteen weeks. Nearly halfway there. Nugget is about the size of a banana right about now."

"Do you know what it is?" I ask dumbly.

"Not yet. I have an anatomy scan soon. Had to locate a new doctor once I got here."

Yeah, we're having this entire conversation while trapped together with a leash. I am a moron.

Still, I find myself unwilling to figure out a way to separate us.

"Does the dog have a name?" she asks.

"I've been calling him Mouse, just because he's pretty skittish."

"Mouse. I can see it." She bites down on her lip and asks. "Think maybe we could work together somehow and see if we can get ourselves untangled?"

"Right! Sorry," I say.

"It's okay. It's just that Nugget is poking at my bladder, and I'd rather not fall on the cement."

"Oh, Daisy, I wouldn't let you fall. I mean, you could fall on me. I'll take the hit to protect you and the baby."

I do what I can to maneuver the leash around, having to unclip it from Mouse's collar.

"Do not run away, you menace," I tell him.

Like the lovesick fool he is, he stays right by Daisy's side.

Finally I get us free and reclip the lead to his collar.

"So, how are you settling into your brother's cabin?"

"It's okay; it's an adjustment. Maybe I'm just not used to being so alone. I had a roommate in my flat in London, and then the first week here, I had to pretend the noises I heard in the cabin weren't my brother and best friend doing naked things together." She touches my arm. "Don't get me wrong, I love that they're together. That they fell in love. It seems like it was inevitable in many ways. But I don't wanna hear them getting it on, ya know?"

I laugh. "Yeah, I get that."

"Anyways, so it's an adjustment and there's a lot of insomnia with pregnancy, so I wake up with every little noise. Then I work myself into a lather about what it could be." She waves a hand. "I'm ridiculous. I'll get used to it. It'll be my new normal." Her hand goes to her belly. "Until this one comes around and turns everything upside down."

"You know, I might have a solution for you. And frankly, it would be a really huge favor for me—not that you were offering to do me a favor, or that I am owed one. But Mouse here, can't really stay at the sanctuary anymore." Mostly because Mouse is my fucking dog. But I leave that part conveniently out. "All of the other dogs make him nervous, and he's just not settling in. Would you be interested in maybe fostering him, and he could stay with you? Just for a little while. Like on a trial basis."

"That would be amazing," she says.

"I mean you did ask him if he wanted to come home with you. Seems only fair that you follow through," I say with a wink.

A goddamn wink.

Since when am I the kind of guy who winks at a woman?

Since Daisy, apparently.

chapter four

DAISY

Beau and Mouse follow me inside Flynn's cabin. "Sorry it's such a mess in here. I just kind of showed up on their doorstep." I say all of this while I'm picking up pieces of my clothing that are literally piled on the single chair in the living room. The couch is bare except for the folded bedding I've been using.

"It's a small place, don't worry about it." He nods to the couch. "You aren't sleeping in the bed?"

My eyebrows nearly climb into my hairline. "Uh, no. Not after all the noises I heard. Vivid imagination and I just couldn't. Even after changing the sheets." I shrug, clutching my clothes to my chest. "I'm weird, I know."

I head down the short hallway to the bedroom and dump my pile of clothes on the bed.

I come back out and find Beau on his knees in front of Mouse. His athletic shorts mold to his ridiculously muscular thighs.

Saliva pools in my mouth. My hormones have been out of control lately and my libido is off the charts. What a great time to be single.

His t-shirt fits across his broad torso like it was made for him. His dark blond hair is once again tucked beneath a backwards ball cap and damned if I don't want to take it off of him and run my fingers through his hair. There are some scars peeking up from the shirt where his shoulders and neck meet.

He notices me standing there and immediately comes to his feet. His hand goes to the back of his head and he rubs. "He's already eaten today so you won't need to feed him. But I can bring some food for you tomorrow."

"That would be great. Will he let me know when he needs to go out?"

Beau nods. "Yeah, he'll uh, go sit by the door."

"What a smart boy," I coo. Mouse ambles over to me on his long legs. "He's so tall and his coat is so unusual looking. Do you know what he is?"

"The vet said likely part Husky and part German Shepherd."

"Oh, that fits. Especially with his eyes." I look down at my new foster friend. "Such a pretty boy, aren't you?"

"Listen, I really appreciate this. You're doing me such a favor."

"Don't mention it. I think Mouse and I will get along very well."

"Is there anything I could do for you? You know in return?" I swear his eyes heat and slowly peruse my body.

I am certain that's not what he's doing and I'm just a dirty, horny little horndog. So before I can ask him for any number of the sexual favors currently scrolling through my brain, I just blurt out, "Not that I can think of." Then I smile.

"Well, think on it and let me know. Should we," he holds his hand out with his phone there, "exchange numbers or whatever?"

"Oh yeah, great idea." I hand him my phone and it dings just as he hands it back to me.

"Now you have my phone number. Feel free to save it under 'handsome devil' or 'the hot one,'" he says.

I laugh. "Sounds good. I'll see you tomorrow, I guess."

"Definitely. Have a good night, Daisy." He glances at the dog. "Keep her safe, Mouse." Then he turns and leaves.

chapter **five**

BEAU

ROMEO: This motherfucker.

EVAN: Who?

ROMEO: <picture of Beau getting in his truck>

ME: Fuck you. Quit taking pictures of me, you stalker.

LIAM: Heh. What did he do?

ROMEO: Left his motherfucking dog with Daisy.

EVAN: Oh shit, you scared me. I thought this was our regular group chat. I take it we're keeping this from Flynn?

ME: Nothing to keep from him. Daisy said she was feeling nervous being in a new town, so I left Mouse there to keep her safe.

LIAM: You just gave her your dog.

ME: Technically, she doesn't know Mouse is my dog.

ROMEO: This oughta be good.

ME: I didn't lie. Mouse hated it at the sanctuary.

EVAN: It's why you adopted him. To get him away from all the noise.

ME: Exactly. Now Daisy is doing the same.

LIAM: You are an idiot.

ME: I don't see how. I left her with a guard dog. It's not like she would have taken him in the cabin if I'd just offered her my dog.

LIAM: Right. Because that's fucking weird.

ME: Whatever. End justifies the means.

ROMEO: What end are you hoping for here, brother?

ME: Just being friendly and offering our buddy's sister a way for her to feel safe. You guys are making this a big deal.

I am one hundred percent lying to myself. I know this. But I still think I made the right choice.

LIAM: Pretty sure you're just lying to yourself.

EVAN: What he said.

ME: Whatever. I bet Flynn will thank me.

ROMEO: I don't think that's what Flynn will be doing, but I'll let you have it for now.

ROMEO: Be careful.

ME: With what?

LIAM: With Daisy! Dumbass. She's not a hit it and quit it kind of girl.

ME: You think I don't know that?

ME: For fuck's sake, she's pregnant.

ME: I was just trying to be a nice guy.

LIAM: All right. I hope that's true. Because if you hurt her Flynn will kill you and make it look like an accident.

LIAM: We'll probably help him.

ME: You guys are the worst.

chapter six

BEAU

I wait until what I think is a reasonable time of the morning to head over to Daisy's. I never sleep well, so I've been up since before the sun rose. But by the time I park my truck by the cabins, it's nearly a quarter after ten. Daisy had mentioned that pregnancy affects sleep, so hopefully I won't be waking her up.

As it turns out, I don't have to worry about it because Daisy is outside with Mouse on his leash. There is an older woman standing near them frowning and talking wildly with her hands.

I do not like the look of whatever is going on.

My stride eats up the space between my truck and the women. When I reach Daisy, I instinctively reach out and put my hand at the small of her back.

"Everything okay?" I ask.

"No!" the older woman snaps. "Everything is not okay. It came to my attention that not only was this young lady staying in one of the cabins without her name being on the lease, but she was doing so with a dog that exceeds the weight limit for pets in these facilities." Somehow the short older lady manages to look down on me.

Considering I'm at least a head taller than her, that seems impressive, if not annoying.

"It's her brother's cabin. She's only staying there temporarily," I explain.

"Mr. Harrington should have sought permission before hand in writing with at least a thirty-day notice."

I stare at the grey-haired tyrant. "Thirty days ago she didn't know she'd be coming back to Texas."

"A policy is a policy, Mr.," she pauses waiting for me to fill in the blank, but I turn away from her to face Daisy.

Her eyes swim in tears and her cheeks are

streaked. What kind of geriatric monster can make a beautiful pregnant woman cry.

"She says that not only can Mouse not stay, but I can't either," Daisy says.

"Do you want me to call your brother?"

Daisy shakes her head. "No, I don't want to involve him in my mess. He's already got his hands full with the estate stuff." Her eyes meet mine and it's like a kick to my solar plexus. "Beau? What am I going to do?"

"I've got you." I wrap my arm around her shoulders and squeeze her close to me. "Let's go get your stuff packed up."

"But where will I go?"

"You're coming home with me. I've got an extra bedroom, and I'm at the sanctuary most of the time, so you'll have the house to yourself. Well, you and Mouse."

"I can't put you out that way. We barely know each other."

"It's not putting me out. Remember, you're helping me with Mouse. Also, your brother would kick my ass if I let you end up homeless."

I have a feeling that ass kicking is coming to me for one reason or another.

Daisy sniffs and nods. "If you're sure."

"I am." I turn my focus on the grey-haired woman. "We'll be out of your hair in twenty minutes. But I want to go on the record as to saying this policy is ridiculous. Also, you made a pregnant woman cry. Did you want to kick her dog too while you're at it?"

I don't give the indignant woman a chance to respond, I turn Daisy and Mouse towards the cabin and we disappear inside.

Nearly two hours later I have both of them settled at my rental house that's nestled on a quiet tree-lined street not too far from downtown. It hasn't been updated in years, but it has great space, and the backyard is perfect for dogs.

By the time I make it out to the sanctuary I'm in a foul mood, still pissed about Daisy effectively being evicted. I storm into Dane's office; the door slams against the opposite wall.

He just raises an eyebrow in response.

"Do you know who owns those rental cabins?"

"Well, a local family owned them for years but sold them about nine months ago, I guess. To some rental management company. Why? You look madder than a wet cat."

"They evicted Daisy," I say. "Some bullshit

about needing a thirty-day notice from the leasee for someone else to sublet."

Dane's office isn't big enough to pace but I'm still prowling around the small space.

"So we need to find somewhere for her to stay?" Dane asks.

"No. I solved that already. I was just hoping there was someone in town I could yell at."

"What do you mean you solved it. Where is she?"

"At my house," I say.

"Because you're clearly a moron or you have a death wish."

I shrug. "It was a problem. I solved it. That's what I do."

"And in true Grenadier form, you're being about as subtle as a wrecking ball."

"It's not a big deal, Dane. I'm out here most of the time. Pretty much just go home to sleep."

"Uh-huh," Dane says, clearly unconvinced. He pinches the bridge of his nose. "Look, Beau, I know you were displaced all the time as a kid, so you can't really appreciate the protectiveness a brother feels over his sister. But surely you realize that you are playing with fire with this girl."

"I'm not going to touch her. I know she's off limits."

"You sure about that?" he asks.

"Yeah. Also, maybe what I'm feeling is that brotherly protectiveness over her."

Dane nods slowly. "Sure. So I guess that means you didn't notice her tits?"

I turn on my buddy, lean forward and brace my hands on his desk. Anger, hot and thick surges through my body and I may or not be breathing fire at this moment.

"Don't you fucking talk about her like that. And keep your fucking eyes to yourself."

He watches me for a moment, then points behind me. "Sit down, Ranger."

I glare at him.

"NOW!"

I reluctantly lower myself into the chair behind me. I cross my arms over my chest. I know my legs are shaking. It's one of the main reasons I was pacing. This much adrenaline needs some kind of outlet. But sitting here, it's just gonna rattle through my legs.

"You gonna talk or just stare at me?" I ask.

"I'm trying to decide how fucked you actually are."

"I don't know what you're talking about."

He spins his wedding band around his finger. "A brother's warning means something," he begins.

I'm about to say something but he holds his hand up to silence me.

"But it doesn't mean everything."

I open my mouth, then close it.

"I've known you a long damn time, Beau. I've seen you with women and they've never meant more than a good time to you. Correct me if I'm wrong."

"You're not," I admit.

He nods. "I was the exact same. Until I wasn't. Until Shelby. Oh, I tried to one and done her—made my pretty girl cry. But I came to my senses, thankfully before I'd fucked everything up beyond repair."

"Why are you telling me this?"

"In case you need someone in your corner."

I narrow my eyes at him.

"If you find that the protectiveness you feel for Daisy isn't so brotherly, then I can help."

"Help with what, exactly?"

He steeples his hands under his chin, and he looks like he's either going to ask me to help with world domination or he's about to drop some wisdom on my ass.

"I know you just met her. And I know she's carrying another man's baby. And she's one of OUR unit member's younger sister. That's a whole hell of a lot of uncertainty. I wouldn't have wanted any of you fuckers near my sister, Daphne. Well, except maybe Evan, he's a sweet kid. But I know you, brother, and there's a different look in your eyes when it comes to Daisy Harrington. I'm not saying something *is* happening between y'all. What I am saying is *if* things move in that direction. If you're ready for something real, something long term. And if she'll have you. I'll help."

I stare at my friend that I've known for years. I wait for some smart-ass remark to bubble out of my mouth, but nothing comes. So I just nod, and say, "Thank you."

"I think for the time being, we should keep Daisy's whereabouts just between us. That's not the kind of thing Flynn needs to hear about when he's up to his eyeballs with legal nonsense."

"Agreed."

Dane stands and holds his hand out to me.

I shake it, then turn to go. But I pause.

“Is it worth it?” I ask, without turning around.

“Is what worth it?”

This time I do glance over my shoulder. “Marriage. The wife, family, cohabitation, all of that?”

“With the right person?” Dane nods. “Absolutely.”

chapter **seven**

DAISY

I can't sleep. Or rather, I'm awake again. Nugget is clearly taking after her Aunt Temple and is doing some aerial yoga in there. And I have to pee. Again.

Poor Mouse is so over me waking him up so often, he's taken to sleeping in the hallway. In the space between my room and Beau's. He lifts his head as I creep out of my room towards the bathroom. When he sees where I am headed, he just lies back down with a doggy sigh.

Tell me about it, pup. This isn't fun for any of us.

After doing my business and washing my hands, I head out to Beau's kitchen in search of a snack. Or at the least some water. Gotta keep hydrating myself considering I go to the bathroom every seven minutes.

My bare feet make little noise on the linoleum floor as I move to the refrigerator. Two days ago when Beau had brought me here—all indignant and fuming on my behalf, he'd got me settled on his sofa with a snack and a movie and had me text him foods that I wanted from the store. Then he'd headed out to the local H-E-B and stocked up.

There were no fewer than four types of Blue Bell ice cream in the freezer. That would likely not help with the heartburn though. I peer into the fridge, taking stock to see if anything jumps out at me.

"Can't sleep either?"

I squeak and jump, then turn to face the direction where Beau's deep voice had come from.

"You scared the hell out of me," I say, my hand over my rapidly beating heart.

He gives me a smile across the LED lit room. His big body perches on one of the chairs at the kitchen table. His blond hair sticks up in every direction, but this is the first time I've seen him without his hat. He's also wearing a tank top that reveals more of his sculpted shoulders and biceps than my middle-of-the-night-pregnant-brain is ready for.

Lord help me, I want to climb that man like a cat in heat.

I turn away, intent on finding myself some water. Maybe I should just pour it over my head though instead of drinking it.

It's gotta be the hormones, right? I mean I've never reacted this strongly to a man before. There's probably some anthropological reason why I look at him and see him as mate material.

Obviously!

Anyone with ovaries would do the same. He's a big, strong, gorgeous man who could clearly protect our cave. Anthropologically, speaking, of course.

"What do you need, Little Mama?"

His voice comes from directly behind me. He started calling me that the day I moved in here, and his voice is so sweet and tender when he says it. I am in way over my head with this man.

The heat from his nearness makes my nipples harden into painful points.

"Water," I croak.

Then he's got a hand on my hip—which I'm now realizing is bare except for panties because I just walked my happy ass out here in nothing but a t-shirt and my underwear. Holy hell, what is the matter with me?

Anyways, big, meaty hand on my hip as he leans forward and around me to grab a glass from the cupboard. He gives my hip a squeeze.

"Go sit down. I'll bring it to you," he says.

I skirt out from under his arm and find my way to the kitchen table. I look up in time to see him walking towards me. Something about the dimness of the kitchen, the time of the night and his bare feet make this moment feel unbelievably intimate.

He hands me the glass of water. "You need anything else?"

I'm about to answer when there's a sharp kick to my ribcage. I wince.

"What's the matter?" he asks, his voice urgent.

"Nothing. Nugget is busy tonight." I gesture

vaguely to my belly. "Doing yoga or parkour or something."

"Does it always hurt?"

I shake my head. "No. Only when they hit an organ or something."

He's hovering, still concerned that I'm being hurt.

"Did you want to..." I leave the rest of the question unsaid because I don't know how to ask. *Did you want to feel up my big belly? How about you put your hands on me?*

He falls to his knees in front of my chair. His hand reaches out, but he's hesitant. So I grab it and move it to where my baby is kickboxing my ribs. The second his hand is pressed to the spot... Kick!

Beau flinches, then he looks up at me. Eyes wide, he keeps his hand on my stomach as my baby repeatedly kicks at him. An impossibly sweet, boyish grin spreads across his face.

"Holy shit," he whispers. "You have a baby in there. Moving around and growing. That's a goddamn miracle, Daisy. You're a miracle."

There's something so earnest and pure in his words that tears spring to my eyes.

Somehow in the movement my tee has

ridden up, exposing a swath of my belly, from my navel to the panty line hidden beneath the swell. In this light it seems like the stretch marks marring my skin are illuminated, like they're fluorescent. I grab at my shirt, trying to cover them.

But Beau's hand stops my progress. "Don't hide yourself from me."

"It's just that I know they're ugly. And they're just going to get worse as the baby grows."

"There's nothing ugly about you, Little Mama, especially not those. You are so beautiful. Every damn inch of you is beautiful."

My throat tightens. "You don't have to say that."

"I don't say things I don't mean." Then he takes my hand and slides it under his shirt, giving me access to his back. His skin is warm, but my fingers meet rough, raised lines—scars that crisscross over his back. Deep and ragged.

I look up at him, not even bothering to hide my tears.

"Foster care wasn't so kind to me," he says. "I don't normally tell people."

"You don't have to tell me anything."

"I'm not going to tonight. I just wanted you

to know that we all have scars. Some more visible than others. You and me, we're both marked by survival." he says.

I swallow thickly and nod.

He looks down at my belly again. His hand settles there like it belongs. Like I belong. And I'm just not quite sure what to do about that.

chapter **eight**

BEAU

I'm done pretending there's not something growing between me and Daisy. I don't know exactly what it is, but I know enough to see that we both feel it.

For the last several nights we've met in the kitchen. Having an insomnia buddy is kind of nice. But it's getting increasingly more difficult to keep my hands off of her. I want to pull her into my lap and kiss the hell out of her. Learn her taste and every curve of her body.

I know that's not my baby growing inside her, but that's not how it feels. I feel just as protective over that little life as I do for my Little Mama.

Tonight when I pad out to the kitchen, she's already in there rummaging through the pantry.

"What are you looking for?" I ask.

She jumps and shrieks. When she turns to face me, she's frowning. "I'm going to have to hang a bell around your neck so you can quit scaring me half to death."

I just smile at her.

"I'm hungry, if you must know. I'd like a cinnamon roll, but obviously we don't have any of those."

"Sit down, Little Mama. I've got you."

She harrumphs but goes and sits at the table.

"While I'm making your snack, tell me what you did today," I say. I pull out the bread I hide—store, whatever—in the freezer. My dirty little secret, plain sliced white bread. No nutritional value, but some things call for it.

"I read in my baby books. Nugget is getting their fingernails and toenails. I ate my weight in antacids. Stupid heartburn."

I go about toasting the slices. While the toaster works, I get out butter and cinnamon and sugar. I make a quick mixture of the two spices and then get down two plates.

"I took a nap. Took Mouse for a walk. Peed about a hundred times. You know, the usual. How about you?"

"We got in some new dogs today. These came from Louisiana. Some shelter that was destroyed with that string of tornados that hit last week. They brought the bulk of the dogs to us."

I butter the toast then sprinkle the mixture over all four slices. Then I bring the plates to the table.

"Want some milk?" I ask.

"Yes, please," she says, already talking around a bite. "Ohmygosh!" she moans.

And just like that, my dick is hard. Fucking spectacular. I try to adjust my shirt so it hangs over most of the tent in my shorts.

"This is so good. Perfect. Exactly what I was craving."

"Good ol' cinnamon toast to the rescue. This was the only thing I could make myself for the longest time. I'm just glad I never got tired of it." I set down the glasses of milk and sit next to her. I resist the urge to pull her to me and just lean into her neck and breathe in her sweet scent.

She grins at me. "Thank you for my snack."

"Of course."

There's a bit of cinnamon and sugar stuck to the corner of her mouth.

"You've got a little," I lean over and swipe it away with my thumb then like a fucking moron, I lick it away.

She sucks in a breath, her eyes locked on my mouth.

"I really want to kiss you," I admit.

"Me too."

"It's probably a bad idea though. Right?"

"Oh, because of the baby." She doesn't look at me as she sits back in her seat. "You're probably right. I mean I do come with a lot of baggage. Not that my baby is baggage, per se—"

I put my finger over her mouth to stop her talking. "It's not about the baby. I just don't want to push you for something you're not ready for or that you don't want."

She nods.

"Also, your brother threatened to pull all of my limbs off if I touched you."

She laughs. "Flynn? I mean he's taller than you, but you have way more muscles. Not that I've been looking at all your muscles."

"You can look at my muscles, Little Mama. Any time you want."

Her attention moves back to her cinnamon toast. After we eat for a bit in silence, she clears her throat. "You said once that you never had a mom or a sister. Then you said you had a rough go of it in foster care. I don't need to know anything you don't want to share. I'm just curious."

"What do you want to know?" I ask.

"Did you ever have a family?"

"Not until I joined the Army. And even then it took until my Ranger unit. Those guys—including your brother—they are my family."

She nods. "Do you want one of your own? Like a wife and kids or whatever?" Then she winces. "That sounds like I'm offering myself up, which I'm not, I truly am just curious."

I scoot my chair closer to hers. "Until recently, no, I never wanted any of those things. Never felt like that sort of thing was an option for a man like me. When you grow up never being picked, you learn pretty quickly that sometimes things are better just on your own."

Her throat bobs as she swallows.

"You're the first pregnant woman I've ever

been this close to. Frankly, I'd never given much thought to any of it." I take a chance and reach out, putting my hand on her stomach. "You've definitely given me a different view of a possible future."

"Would you take me to the doctor tomorrow? It's the ultrasound for the anatomy scan, and I'm nervous. I'd rather not go alone."

"I'll take you anywhere you want to go, Daisy. You need only ask."

chapter nine

DAISY

I've barely been back in my bed for about forty minutes when I know something isn't quite right. I recognize that the thunder is louder back here than it was in the kitchen. Not to mention the lightning is creating strobe effects across the old, flowered wallpaper.

The rain itself is what sounds louder though. Like I can hear the drip, drip, drip of it hitting something metal.

Drip.

Drip.

Drip.

Plop.

That one I felt right on my face. My eyes search the darkened ceiling. Where's that flash of lightning when you need it?

Plop.

Another, then another, hitting my face. I sit up. Now the drops are hitting my pillow.

Okay, clearly dealing with a roof leak.

I crawl out of bed and try to flick the lights on, but nothing happens. Power must be out as well. I creep out into the hall and Mouse lifts his head to stare at me.

"Hey sweet boy," I whisper to him. "It's raining in my room."

"Little Mama," Beau's voice comes from his room. "What's the matter?"

I go stand in his doorway, and he's sitting up in bed, shirtless. Why does he have to be so damn attractive?

"Don't worry about me," I say. "I'll figure something out. Just go back to sleep."

"Don't be dumb. Get your pretty little ass over here." He holds up the covers.

I only hesitate for a moment before I step into his room. His King size bed is bigger than average so there's plenty of room for us to share.

Once I sink into the bed, I'm surrounded by the masculine scent of Beau. I release a happy sigh and settle into the pillow.

"I love all your little noises," he murmurs into the darkness.

With us both in this room, Mouse comes inside and plops down at the far end so he can keep a protective eye on both of us. He really is just the best dog.

"I'll get started on fixing the roof in the morning. Hopefully, I won't find any other patches," Beau says. His sleepy voice feels intimate, but there's nothing about being in his bed that gives me pause. If anything, it feels like this is where I'm supposed to be.

"Get some sleep, Little Mama, we've got to get you to your doctor's appointment tomorrow," he says.

Somehow my body obeys, and I manage to fall into a deep sleep.

chapter ten

BEAU

I wake to the sound of a moan.

My senses come to one at a time.

A hot body presses against mine.

Rain patters on the windows behind my bed.

The sweet scent of fruity shampoo wafts around me.

Another moan.

That one might have been mine.

My dick is a lead pipe in my boxer briefs.

Daisy. Daisy is in my bed because her ceiling was leaking. I open my eyes to find her body wrapped around mine. Her thighs are spread, and she's managed to find my erection since I'm angled towards her.

I think she's still asleep, but her sweet pussy is grinding against me.

Fuck, that's hot.

As hot as it is, I want her awake for this. If she's going to make herself come, I want her to know it's me who's under her.

"Daisy," I whisper her name.

I shift our bodies so I'm lying flat on my back and she's straddling me. That manages to jar her awake. Her eyes are wide when she realizes where she is.

My hands tighten on her hips. I rock my pelvis up and my cotton-covered cock rubs against her core. Even through her underwear and mine, I can feel the heat of her pussy.

"Use me. Get yourself off. You were doing it in your sleep. Rubbing your sweet cunt all over me. Make yourself come, Daisy. Do it."

Her mouth closes and she swallows. I half expect her to roll off of me, but she doesn't. Instead, she braces her hands on my chest and starts to move. She whimpers as she rocks, and she is the sexiest thing I've ever seen in my life.

Right here in my bed, basically fully clothed, pregnant with another man's baby. She is gorgeous.

I know in that moment that I want her next orgasm. I want to watch it, knowing I helped in some small way. But I'm a greedy motherfucker, and I want all of the rest of them too. Every last orgasm wrung from her body, I want to own them.

"That's it, Mama, you rub yourself all over my hard cock. Fuck! Can you feel how much I want you?"

She nods, making a non-word noise in the back of her throat.

Her nipples are hard and poking at the fabric of her t-shirt. I reach up to cup her, but I pause before actually touching her.

"Can I play with your tits?" I ask.

"Yes, please. My nipples are so sensitive. Oh my God, Beau. You feel so good."

I feel the weight of her big tits against my palms and swipe my thumbs over her turgid tips.

She releases a strangled cry and arches into my touch. All the while her pussy works across my dick.

I pinch her nipples, tug at them lightly.

"Shit, I'm going to come," she breathes. Then she does, breaking against me and crying out my name.

We haven't even kissed yet, but I know what she sounds like when she comes with my name on her lips.

This woman is going to end me. Everything I thought I knew about the world seems fuzzy. Like it's all in transition. When I get through to the other side, I'll have a new understanding of everything that is. She will be the center of it all.

She sags against me. Then seems to come to her senses. Her body rolls to her side of the bed. "This trimester has made me unabashedly horny," she says. "I've had more than one vivid sex dream. But normally I'm in bed alone. Though I've woken up, on more than one occasion, with my hand in my panties."

"You don't owe me an explanation."

"I just used your body to get myself off."

"Yeah. And it was hot as fuck." I lean up on my elbow and look at her. "But you know what I think?"

"What's that?"

"I think you need one more. One that'll

really wring you out so you can sleep until morning."

Her lips part. "I see."

"Can I eat you, Daisy? Can I lick your pussy until you come all over my face?"

"Yes, please. That sounds outstanding."

I chuckle, then stand from the bed. I know my scars are on full display as I turn and walk around to her side. But I don't feel like hiding in front of her anymore.

I get on the bed, sniper position, and wedge my shoulders between her thighs.

"I've never come this way," she admits.

"Good. Then you'll only remember how I did it for you." She's got a sizable wet spot at the front of her cotton panties. I lean forward and breathe her in. "You smell so good." I pull the fabric to the side and get my first glimpse of her swollen pink parts. It's still dark in here, but my eyes have adjusted enough to see that it's the prettiest pussy I've ever seen.

I lean forward and lick her from slit to clit.

Her back arches.

"Tell me if I do anything you don't like."

She nods, then her head falls back to the pillow.

I use my tongue to clean up her last climax, licking her clean. I can get her there with her panties still on, me holding them away from her sensitive flesh. But I want her to be able to move. So I grab the fabric and rip it at the seams, then toss it on the floor.

"Did you just rip my panties off?"

"They were in my way."

"I love that."

Like this, I can put my hands beneath her ass and tilt her upwards to my mouth. I devour her. Licking and sucking, my tongue is everywhere.

She's writhing and moaning. Her nails scrape against my scalp as she threads her fingers into my hair.

"Beau. Oh wow, that feels unbelievable. So good. It's so good. Don't ever stop."

"I'm never going to fucking stop. Never," I growl at her, then go back to eating her. She's the most delicious thing I've ever had in my mouth. I rock myself against the mattress, trying to get some pressure on my hard cock.

I move one hand from under her so I can slide some fingers inside her slick channel. With me finger fucking her, I concentrate my mouth on her needy little clit. I slow my fingers and press them to the front wall of her pussy. Then I move them back and forth.

"Oh my hell," she yells. "I think I'm going to come."

I suck her clit into my mouth and rub those fingers against her G-spot.

"Yes, yes! Oh my God!"

Her orgasm crashes over her and her body trembles. She comes directly into my mouth and I lick up her release.

"Did I just pee?" she asks, her voice shrill.

"No. You just squirted. Right in my fucking mouth too."

"Should I apologize?"

"Never. It was the hottest fucking thing ever. Made me come in my boxers." I give her pussy a sweet kiss, then climb up from the bed. I walk to my dresser and grab another pair of boxers. I drop my wet ones and then walk to the bathroom. "Wait there, beautiful. I'm going to get something to clean you off."

"You have a really spectacular ass, Beau Stevens," she says.

I chuckle. "Thank you." I clean myself off, then put on the new boxers. "You have a really spectacular everything, Daisy Harrington."

If I knew for certain that beneath the bone and sinew and skin of my chest beat an actual heart, I'd know it belonged to her. But am I really enough for this amazing woman?

Probably not.

chapter eleven

DAISY

We woke up late.

The two insomniacs who've had clandestine midnight kitchen meetings since we've been cohabitating, overslept. We woke up not wrapped up in each other, like you read about in some books. But somehow we were holding hands.

I wasn't sure how the morning would go after me sleep molesting him last night and then him eating me out like it was an Olympic sport. He legitimately won the Gold, just so we're clear on that.

I'm not one to compare lovers. Especially since I've had exactly two and Beau and I haven't even had actual sex yet. But Timothy went down on me a few times and he was so persnickety about everything—the taste, the smell, the hair. It made me self-conscious and I never could get into it. I probably should have known then that he was a selfish ass.

But I'd just assumed that guys who really enjoyed that sort of thing only lived in romance novels.

I glance over at Beau's profile. We're sitting in the waiting room at the doctor's office. Beau's legs jiggle as he sits and looks around at all the diagrams on the wall of the female reproductive system.

"You could have waited in your truck," I tell him. "I'm sorry if this is making you uncomfortable."

He looks at me. "I'm not uncomfortable. Did you want me to go wait outside? You had mentioned being nervous, so I guess I assumed you wanted me to go in there with you."

"That is what I wanted. But only if it's not weird for you."

He cups my face and gives me a sweet smile

and holy dimples, Batman, I am in so much trouble. My stupid, stupid heart is falling for this big guy, but this is a non-starter.

No man is going to want to hitch his wagon to my proverbial cart. Especially when I'm having another man's baby.

This thing between me and Beau is clearly just insane sexual chemistry.

"Daisy Harrington," the technician calls from the doorway.

I stand and hold my hand out to Beau. I do want him in there with me. I'm tired of trying to be brave all the time and do all of this alone. There will be plenty of time later for me to buck up and be a good single mom. Right now I want at least the illusion of having a partner.

He threads our fingers together and we follow the tech back to the exam room. It's a special room for the 3D scanner.

The lights in the ultrasound room are dimmed low, a soft glow surrounding the high-tech equipment. I lie back on the exam table, tugging my shirt up over the curve of my belly. Beau sits down beside me and takes my hand again like it's the most natural thing in the world.

The technician—a kind-looking woman

with silver-framed glasses and a calming voice—smiles as she pulls on gloves.

"Alright, we're going to take a look at your little one today. Dad, are you ready?"

Beau stiffens for half a second, then glances at me. I expect him to correct her. But he doesn't, instead he nods.

"Yes, ma'am," he says, voice gravelly but warm. "Been ready."

My chest squeezes tight. I don't look at him, I can't.

Cool gel smears across my skin, making me shiver. The wand presses down, and suddenly the screen flickers to life with grainy gray movement.

"There's baby," the tech says. She clicks and scans, clicks and scans again. "So far, everything is measuring just right."

Beau leans forward, his eyes wide. "That's... that's the baby? That little thing's moving so much already? No wonder you can't sleep at night."

The tech chuckles. "That's your baby kicking up a storm." She moves the wand and Nugget does some kind of ninja move. The tech laughs again. "Somebody's got a lot of energy."

Beau lets out a low, astonished laugh, and I

feel it rumble through his chest, where our arms are brushing. "She's doing somersaults in there," he murmurs, his voice clearly in awe.

"She?" I ask him.

He shrugs. "She feels like a she."

"So you're not seeing something on there that I'm not, right?" I ask, searching the gray static-filled screen again.

The tech moves the wand, narrating as she goes. "Here's the spine. Look at that beautiful alignment. And the heart—all four chambers looking good, Mom. Definitely a strong, fast heartbeat."

She hits a button and suddenly the room fills with the whoosh-whoosh of my baby's heartbeat. Tears prick at my eyes.

"Whoa. That is fast," Beau whispers.

"Perfectly normal," the tech says. "Strong and steady. That's what we like to see. And here's the profile—look at that nose! Dad, she's got your chin."

Beau blinks, startled. "Mine?" His eyes are locked on the screen as he looks at my baby's sweet profile.

The tech keeps going, naming off femurs, stomach, kidneys, a perfectly curved skull. Beau never looks away. His mouth parts slightly, and he's got this expression—like he's witnessing something sacred.

"Do we want to know the sex? Because I think we're in a perfect position to see," the tech says.

"Yes, please," I say.

The screen shifts again, the tech clicks and the image freezes. It's like looking up at the baby from below. "See these two lines that look like an equal sign?" the tech asks.

I nod.

"Well, it looks like Dad was right. You're definitely having a girl."

Beau makes this sound, half laugh, half choke. He scrapes his hat off his head and runs a hand through his hair, then puts the hat back on.

"A girl," I echo.

"Is that what you wanted?" Beau asks.

Before I can answer though, the tech has printed out a series of pictures for us and is clicking away on the machine. "Congratulations," she says. "Your daughter looks absolutely perfect."

My daughter.

The tech hands me a towel to clean off my

belly and then tells me I'm done. She closes the door as she leaves the room.

Beau looks over at me, and I can't even describe what's in his eyes—something reverent, like I'm holy and terrifying all at once. He lifts my hand and presses his lips to my knuckles.

"You made a girl," he murmurs. "A whole little girl."

I shake my head, overwhelmed. It's on my tongue to remind him that my baby is half of Timothy's, but I don't even want to mention his name in this moment.

"She's yours," he says fiercely. "She's gonna be the best damn thing that ever happened to this world."

chapter twelve

BEAU

I hold her hand all the way to my truck.

I feel reborn in a way I don't understand. All I know is that seeing Daisy's daughter with her tiny toes and fluttering heart and that sweet, sweet profile, changed me. I am not the same man that walked into that office.

By the time we reach my truck, my blood feels like it's humming through my veins. Vibrating on a new frequency.

Before I open Daisy's door, I press her against it.

"That was amazing. Thank you for sharing it with me."

She looks up into my face and she's so goddamn beautiful, everything inside me cracks open. I lower my mouth to hers and finally taste her. Her lips part immediately, and her arms come up around my neck. Then she's kissing me back.

With every press of her lips, every swipe of her tongue, the broken parts inside of me piece back together.

Our kiss deepens, and we are likely being obscene for a parking lot in Saddle Creek. But I can't get enough of this woman.

I pull back, far enough to press my forehead to hers.

"If we don't stop, I'm going to fuck you right here in the parking lot. I want you too goddamn much," I say.

"Home," she manages.

And that's all I need to know. I help her up into the truck, then race to the other side. I don't dare touch her on the drive back to my rental house because I don't trust myself not to just pull to the side of the road and lose myself inside her.

"Fuck, Little Mama," I say, my voice rough, "I'm so damn hard for you, I'm surprised my dick hasn't drilled through my zipper.

She reaches over and presses her palm to the front of my jeans. "My panties are soaked," she admits.

By the time I hit my driveway and park under my carport, I am half out of my mind for want of her.

"Stay put," I tell her. When I open her door she tries to step out, but instead I pick her up, cradling her to my chest like she's my bride. Like I get to keep her.

I shove those thoughts away. If she'll have me, I'll stay with her in whatever capacity she'll let me. Her and her daughter.

I march us straight into my bedroom, not even bothering to peek into the backyard and check on Mouse. Nothing matters more in this moment than Daisy. I set her down on the bed and immediately start taking off my clothes.

Then I pause. "Shit," I murmur.

She's halfway out of her shirt. "What's the matter?" she asks.

"I just remembered that I don't have a condom. I haven't needed any in a while. Haven't been with a woman in a long damn time." I haven't admitted that to any of the guys. I'm sure they all still think I'm hitting the bars every weekend and bringing home a new woman. But the appeal of one-night stands faded before I even got back stateside.

She pulls her shirt the rest of the way off but holds it against her chest. "Well, you can't get me pregnant."

"I'm clean, Little Mama, I promise you."

"I trust you," she says. "I'm clean too. They checked me for everything when I found out asshole Timothy had been sleeping with his wife at the same time as me. So even though I was an idiot, my daughter is the only thing that came out of that mess."

I cup her face. "You are not an idiot. You should never have to wonder if a man is being faithful to you. You are everything, Daisy. If that dumb motherfucker couldn't see it, then he's the goddamn idiot."

She kisses me. And we finish getting undressed in between our heated kisses.

Her hand tries to fist my cock, but her fingers don't quite meet. "You touch me too much, beautiful, and you're going to have me coming before I'm inside of you. I've never been this hard before. Never wanted—needed—anyone the way I need you."

I run my hands down her curves, wrap my palms beneath the weight of her stomach.

"I don't want to hurt her," I admit.

"You won't."

"Are you sure I'm not going to like poke her in the head or something?"

Daisy laughs. "No, there's stuff in there in between my vagina and my uterus."

"I should have paid closer attention in health class, I guess. I was mostly concerned with learning how to use rubbers so I could avoid this situation."

"I think that's what most of us got out of health class," she says.

I take a step back to look at her naked body. "You're the sexiest woman I've ever seen," I say.

"I feel like the sexiest when you look at me."

"So what position will work best because I don't want to put my weight on you? I don't want to do anything that could hurt you or her."

"I can be on top, like last night. Or you can take me from behind."

I squeeze my eyes shut and squeeze the root

of my dick. "I'm going to do everything I can to not nut too early, but you are driving me insane, Little Mama."

Her head tilts. "Do you have a pregnancy kink?"

I shake my head. "No, I have a Daisy kink." I tweak her nipples. "Now get up on that bed on all fours."

"Yes," she hisses and moves to obey my command.

Like this I can see all of her. The heavy weight of her tits hanging. The curve of her waist that almost disappears completely from some angles. The rounded belly that houses that perfect little miracle. Her plump ass and thick thighs.

"Yeah, you, Little Mama," I say running my hand up the curve of her ass to her neck. "You are my kink. This, seeing you like this, this is my porn. Goddamn, you're sexy."

She wiggles. "I'm making a mess on my thighs. Please Beau. Fuck me."

I reach between her legs and find she's not lying about the mess. She's drenched. I shift my body and rub my cock through her moisture, coating myself. Then I press the head of my dick to her entrance.

"It might be harder to take you if I wasn't so turned on. Because you are bigger than Timothy in every way."

That unleashes some sort of primal urge, and I thrust forward, bottoming out inside her. My balls slap up against her body, and she moans.

"Too much?" I ask.

"No. It's perfect."

I grip her hips and start to pump myself inside her. Nothing has ever felt so good. Not the first time I tugged myself to climax. Not the first time I sank into a woman. No blow job or toy or anything. There is nothing that compares to the wet heat and the tight grip of Daisy.

She lowers down on her elbows, which lets me sink deeper.

"Faster," she breaths. "Every time you slide back in your balls hit my clit."

"You're perfect," I grit.

"Keep going. You're totally going to make me come," she whines.

I try to keep my rhythm stable and try not to grip her hips too hard. But I'm losing my ability to think.

"Yes, Beau, right there. Oh shit!" She comes and her body squirms away from me. She squirts again. "Oh fuck, I did it again. You must be magic."

I chuckle. "I think we're just magic together." I lie on the bed and pat my thighs. "Now ride me til I come. I want to be looking in your eyes when I do."

She straddles me, reaching between her legs to notch me in the right position. She slides her pussy all the way down on me and I know my life will never be the same. I'll either need to fuck her or my hand for the rest of my life. Because no other woman will ever feel right.

She rocks back and forth, but my impatience takes hold. I grab her ass and lift her, fucking up into her.

"Oh wow. Your body is insane," she says.

"It's not going to take me long, Daisy. Goddamn it you feel good."

"Take what you need," she says. Her hands rub up my stomach onto my chest. She meets my upward thrust with a downward one of her own.

"I'm going to fucking come," I yell.

"Do it. Give it to me."

I unleash inside of her, and somehow that

manages to set her off again, pulling the rest of my climax from me with the squeezes of her own.

Then she collapses on top of me. I bury my face in her neck, breathing in her hair, her skin, every part of her. I'm pretty sure this is as close as I'll ever get to heaven.

chapter thirteen

BEAU

I wake to the sound of my phone chiming. Then again. And again.

"Somebody wants your attention this morning," Daisy says from next to me.

I love that she's still naked, her voice sleepy, but amused.

I grab my phone and see it's the group chat.

FLYNN: MOTHERFUCKER!

FLYNN: I think I was pretty fucking clear that my sister was off limits!

EVAN: Oh, shit.

ROMEO: Saw this coming from several miles away.

My heart is pounding as the messages roll in.

FLYNN: You made the town gossip rag. Hope you're happy about that.

FLYNN: <img of me kissing Daisy against my truck>

"Oh fuck," I murmur.

"What's the matter?" Daisy asks.

"Your brother. He knows."

She sits up, the sheet pooling at her waist, baring her breasts to me.

"What's he saying?"

I angle the phone so she can see.

. . .

DANE: Remember our conversation, B. Offer still stands.

LIAM: I do not have time for y'all's drama.

ROMEO: Grumpy fuck. You know I'm the actual old one in our group.

FLYNN: I am going to rip your head off when I get home.

EVAN: When is that going to be? Asking for a friend. Who wants to video tape such an event.

"It's none of his business. I am an adult," Daisy says.

"I know, beautiful. But there is a code among men, and I broke it." I hug her to me so her head lays on my chest. "If he has to beat on me, I'll let him."

JACK: Oh damn, you walk away from your phone for five minutes.

DANE: This town's gossip mill is more sophisticated than any spy network.

DANE: Secrets never stay secrets.

FLYNN: Beau!

FLYNN: I'm changing your name in my phone to MOTHERFUCKER.

FLYNN: You have anything to say for yourself, MOTHERFUCKER?

ME: We'll talk when you get home.

FLYNN: Nothing to talk about. Unless you want an opinion about which way I am going to kick your ass.

"He is ridiculous," Daisy says. "I've lived in London for the better part of the last two years, and in that time he married my best friend and then fell in love with her! He doesn't get to have an opinion about my love life."

"I tried to stay away from you," I admit.

That makes her smile. "But you just couldn't?"

"Nope."

"I like that about you," she says. She crawls out of the bed, and I enjoy the sight of her naked body as she goes into the bathroom.

I grab my phone, and send off a single text.

ME: I don't really know where she stands. But from my perspective, I'd like to ask for that help now.

DANE: You've got it.

chapter fourteen

DAISY

A few hours later, Beau and I are getting ready to take Mouse for a walk.

I'm still pissed at my brother. I'm ready to go to battle on Beau's behalf even if our night was a one-time thing. Which I'm guessing that's what this is. I mean judging from the fact that Beau didn't try to explain anything to Flynn.

I finish pulling my hair up in a ponytail and then step out into the living room.

"Are you ready?" I ask.

Beau holds up Mouse's leash. "We just have

to make sure we steer clear of the corgis' house. They make Mouse very nervous."

I scratch Mouse's head. "Those tiny dogs are mean to you, huh, baby? We'll protect you."

We make it to the door, and Beau swings it open. And my past stands there on the porch.

"Well, isn't this domestic," Timothy says, his posh British accent making every syllable sound pretentious and judgmental.

"What the hell are you doing here?" I ask.

Mouse growls, low and deep in his throat.

"Is that?" Beau asks.

"Yep."

Beau hands me the leash. "Go inside. I've got this." He steps out onto the porch.

I'm not going inside because I'm nosy as hell and want to see what's going to happen. I don't have anything to say to Timothy. I got all I needed when he gave me that lump sum of money and signed away his parental rights.

"I don't believe you and I have any business, sir," Timothy says.

"Oh, but we really do," Beau snarls.

"I made a mistake, Daisy. Please forgive me."

"What's the matter, Timothy? Did your wife kick you out?" I ask.

"I just want another chance with you," Timothy pleads.

I look him up and down and wonder what the hell I ever saw in him. Once upon a time he'd been charming and handsome and so romantic. But it had all been a charade.

"You don't deserve another chance," Beau says, his voice is low and deadly. "You don't even deserve to look at her, let alone breathe the same air as her."

"Oh, and I suppose you think you deserve her?" Timothy asks Beau.

"No. I know I don't deserve her. But I also know that no one will take care of her the way I will. No one will ever love her and her baby the way I will."

I think my heart stops beating. He doesn't mean that. Right? I mean he's just saying that to Timothy to make him go away.

"That is not your child," Timothy says.

"It's not yours either, motherfucker," Beau says. "Since you already signed your rights away."

"Daisy, can you call off your beast?" Timothy asks.

"I don't think I will," I say. "I'm rather enjoying this."

"Does this man speak for you?" the sperm donor asks.

"I said everything I needed to say to you back in London. We have nothing to discuss." I put my hand on my stomach, trying to protect my daughter from hearing anything out of Timothy's mouth. "I am not your concern. My child is not your concern. I can't imagine why you would have spent the money to fly yourself all the way to Texas for this ridiculous display."

"Backwater state," Timothy murmurs.

"You had your chance with her. You threw it away," Beau says. "I should kick your ass up and down this street. But I think your pencil dick and that nasal-quality of your voice is probably punishment enough." He takes a step towards Timothy. "Now get the fuck off my property."

"Do not contact me again," I say. "Or I'll be forced to take legal actions." I have no clue if that's even an option, but it sounds good in that moment.

Timothy opens his mouth like he's going to say something, but Beau takes another step towards him. "Whatever it is you think you need to stay, don't. Just walk to your fancy town-car and go back where you came from."

There's a pause and then the sperm donor turns and stalks to his car without another word.

We stand in silence as the black sedan drives away.

I'm not sure what to say to Beau now. Do I tell him I know he wasn't making promises or declarations, that he was only protecting me?

Finally, Beau turns to face me. "You alright?" he asks.

I nod.

"I could've kicked his ass, but I figured you'd prefer I not be violent."

"Probably best that way. Though if anyone ever deserved an ass kicking..."

"I'd wager he got a few growing up," Beau says with a smirk.

That makes me smile.

He steps closer to me. "So I need you to know," he starts.

I brace myself for him to admit that he was just saying things that sounded good in the moment.

"I realize that just because I'm choosing you doesn't mean you're choosing me in return," he says. "I've never done anything like this before, and I fully admit I have no idea what I'm doing.

But I do know, with a certainty in my bones, that I will never not want you. I will never stop hoping that someday maybe you'll feel a fraction for me of what I feel for you."

I look up at his beautiful face and smile. "What are you saying, Beau?"

"I'm saying that I know it's fast and I can't make any sense of it, but I know what I feel. I'm in love with you, Daisy Harrington. I don't ever want to be away from you from this day forward."

He closes the distance between us, but instead of kissing me, his hands go to my bump.

"I'm saying that I have no idea how to be a father since the only one I ever knew did nothing but mark my body. But I'm a fast learner, and once I'm dedicated, I'm all in. No looking back. No regrets. I love both of you, and I'd be so fucking honored if you'd let me be a part of y'all's lives."

I cup his face. "Of course I choose you, you beautiful, sweet man."

"Well, fuck," Flynn's voice comes from behind Beau.

I was so lost in Beau's admission that I didn't even hear my brother and Temple arrive.

Beau spins to see his friend.

"I can't very well beat on you after an admission like that." He steps forward, using those extra few inches he has on Beau's height. "Just promise me you meant it."

"Every fucking word," Beau says.

"Babe, I think you're ruining their special moment," Temple whispers not so quietly from behind Flynn. She looks around my brother's stupid body and gives me a wink.

"I thought I was going to have to kick his ass," Flynn says.

"You still can," Beau says. "I mean I did pursue her. I convinced her to foster Mouse and ended up getting her evicted from your cabin."

"What do you mean she fostered Mouse?" Flynn asks. "That's your dog."

I look up at Beau, brows raised. "That explains so much about Mouse's behavior."

"Sorry I lied, Little Mama. But you stood on that sidewalk and told me you were afraid of being by yourself and weren't sleeping. It was the only thing I could think of. I knew you wouldn't just take my dog."

I throw my arms around his neck and pepper

his face with kisses. "That's the sweetest thing ever. I love you too, you know."

"Yay, happy endings all around," Temple says.

"Wait, does this mean I'm evicted from my cabin?" Flynn asks.

"We'll figure it out," Temple says, grabbing his hand. "Life is an amazing adventure."

"A very unexpected and wonderful adventure," I say, looking up into the eyes of the man I love.

chapter fifteen

BEAU

EVAN: Did I miss it? I'm gonna be pissed if I missed it.

LIAM: Missed what?

EVAN: Beau's ass kicking.

ME: Ass kicking?

ME: What are you talking about.

ME: Flynn is here with me now. He's the big spoon to my little spoon.

FLYNN: For fuck's sake.

FLYNN: For the record, I am spooning my wife.

EVAN: So there was no ass kicking?

EVAN: Y'all suck.

ROMEO: I'll kick your ass, Evan, if you really need me to.

LIAM: Now, that, I would watch.

JACK: Why must we have these group chats at all hours of the day?

DANE: Because they don't have warm, willing women to spend their time with.

FLYNN: Some of us do.

LIAM: While we're all here, I'm leaving town for a few days.

ROMEO: Everything okay?

LIAM: I'm getting married.

EVAN: Say what, now?

ME: Have you been secretly dating someone?

FLYNN: Not everyone dates in secret.

ME: For the record, we haven't even been on an official date. We were just cohabitating.

FLYNN: That does not make me feel better.

ME: I plan to remedy that very soon.

EVAN: There could still be a fight.

ROMEO: Kids! Be quiet and let the adults talk. Liam, details.

LIAM: An old friend. Widow of an even older friend.

LIAM: Custody issue.

LIAM: We're meeting in Vegas.

LIAM: I'll have more details when we get back.

ROMEO: Is this a good thing?

LIAM: It's complicated.

LIAM: But it's the right thing.

EVAN: Another one bites the dust.

EVAN: That just leaves me and you, Romeo.

ROMEO: I'm not marrying you, kid.

ME: Good luck.

LIAM: Thanks.

ME: Daisy and I are official.

DANE: I knew you were different.

FLYNN: It's annoying that he loves her.

FLYNN: I really wanted to kick his ass.

ME: But I do love her. More than anything.

FLYNN: I can't kick his ass when he's being good to my sister. But if he steps out of line.

EVAN: I'll hold him down.

ROMEO: Bloodthirsty much, kid?

JACK: Seriously. Evan, you're our medic. What happened to do no harm?

EVAN: If I'm not the one harming someone, then it's fair game.

ROMEO: You need to get out more.

DANE: Just be patient. Saddle Creek has a festival about every three weeks.

ME: Really?

DANE: Not quite, but it feels like that sometimes.

DANE: Small towns in Texas gotta celebrate everything.

ROMEO: I'm going back to bed. See you fuckers at work later.

bonus epilogue

DAISY

one month later...

“I cannot believe we’re actually married,” I say. Beau wraps his arms around me, pulling me into an embrace.

“It’s true. Are you sure you don’t want the whole big dress, church wedding thing? Because we can still do it,” he says.

I wrap my arms around his neck and smile up at him. “Nope. Having our friends there was all I need. Now, I am officially Mrs. Beau

Stevens and that's good enough for me. And you made an honest woman of be before Nugget comes."

"Thank you for letting me give her my last name." He kisses my forehead, then my cheeks, then my mouth.

"I wouldn't have it any other way."

"We can still have a party too," he says.

"Maybe we should have one with Temple and Flynn since they got married without us around."

"Anything you want, Little Mama."

"There is something I want."

"Tell me and I'll make it happen."

I turn and give him my back. "Can you help me get out of this dress?"

"My pleasure."

"But no touching yet. I have a plan."

He leans forward, his hot breath flutters over my sensitive neck. "My wife has a plan?"

"She does."

"Is this a wifely thing?" he asks.

His hands unzip my pale lavender dress. Not a traditional wedding dress, but then I'm not a traditional bride. And I fell in love with this dress on sight. He pushes the cap sleeves down my arms, and the rest of it falls off my body to pool at my feet. I step out of it.

Beau picks it up and drapes it over the chair on the other side of our bedroom.

I step over to the dresser and grab one of my hair ties. Then I turn and face him and pull all of my long blonde hair up into a ponytail.

He smiles at me. “I like this view, wife.”

“Of me wearing my pregnancy lingerie?”

“Fuck yeah, Little Mama. You are so damn sexy.”

“I’m glad you think so.” I walk towards him, trying to put a a little extra in my hips movement. “Now then, husband. Would you be so kind as to hand me one of those pillows.” I point to the bed.

His eyes narrow, but he does as I ask. “What are you up to?”

“Something that is long overdue. And something I’ve wanted to do for a while.”

He hands me the pillow.

I drop it at my feet, then get down on my knees on it. I look up at him, doing my best to look sexy and not like I’m about to sneeze.

“I know that painting my lips all up in bright red lipstick would make this even sexier, but I’ve always hated lipstick. Don't like the way it tastes or how it feels on my mouth."

"I like your mouth just the way it is," he says.

My hands go to his belt and I unfasten it.

"Daisy," he says my name full of so much adoration. "You don't need to do this."

"I know that. I want to."

"What is it that you want to do?" he asks with a teasing grin.

"Are you trying to get me to talk dirty to you?"

"Maybe I just want to hear you say it."

I stare up into his face. "I want to suck my husband's cock."

"Fuck," he hisses.

I pull down the zipper and shove his pants off of his hips. Then I'm met with the sizable tent he's making in his boxer briefs.

"Already so hard, husband?"

"For you? Always."

I take him out, tucking his boxers beneath his balls. I wiggle my head to make my ponytail move. "You can hold on to me with that if you want."

"I don't want to make you gag."

"You can still guide me or just hold on to

my hair as I do it." I lick my lips, then lean forward. I swipe my tongue up the root of his dick until I get to that sensitive part just under the head.

"Goddamn it, Lille Mama."

I circle the mushroom shaped head with my tongue, never taking my eyes off him.

He takes my hair, wrapping the gathered strands around his hand.

"Look at my sexy as fuck wife, on her knees sucking me. What did I ever do to deserve you?"

"You loved me. No questions asked. And you didn't ask for anything in return," I tell him. "How could I not fall in love with you?"

He smirks. "You forgot to mention my devilish good looks."

"And this big dick," I say, then I suck him all the way into my mouth.

"Daisy, shit!"

I hollow my cheeks as I bob on his cock, swirling my tongue as I go.

He's swearing and moaning and doing his best not to buck his pelvis towards me.

I've never had a particularly sensitive gag reflex. So I loosen my throat and take him as far as I can.

"You're too fucking good at this. I'm not going to last."

I hum around him, then reach up to fondle his balls.

"If you don't want me coming down your throat, wife, you better pop off my dick. Because I'm so damn close."

I'm not going anywhere. I want his saltiness in my mouth. I'm so wet right now, I've probably ruined my fancy wedding panties. But isn't that what they're for.

"Fuck, I'm coming," he grinds out.

Then the warm spurts of his release hits my tongue and throat. I swallow him down as he continues to pulse, all the while whispering my name like a prayer.

He pulls me to my feet, holding me against his chest. "I love you, Daisy Stevens. I love you today, tomorrow and every day after that."

epilogue

BEAU

About 20 weeks later...

I stare at Daisy. Sweaty, messy bun toppling over to the side of her head, dark circles under her eyes, but the sweetest smile on her lips. She's never looked more beautiful.

She tilts her head up for a kiss. I press my lips to hers, then lean down and press a kiss to the baby's downy soft head. She's suckling at her mother's breast, and I'm hit all over again with a wave of such intense love, I don't know what to do with myself.

"I think if I cry any more today, they're going to take my man card away," I say.

Daisy laughs. "Not on my watch."

I rub a finger across the baby's soft cheek. "She's so perfect."

"She really is."

"I wish she was mine." The words fall out of my mouth before I can stop them. I've thought them so many times over the last few months. Through every hard step of Daisy's pregnancy.

"Beau, love, she is yours. You were the one there every night for my cravings. You were the one there at every doctor's appointment. You were the one by my side in the birthing classes. It's why I named her Bella. Your names mean the same thing."

I suck in a breath. "I hadn't realized."

"Yeah. She is as much yours as she is mine. We'll make it legal as soon as we can."

"You mean—" I can't even finish the question.

Daisy nods. "You can legally adopt her. Your name is already on her birth certificate because you're my husband. But we'll go through the whole process. You are her dad in every way that truly counts."

"I love you so damn much, Little Mama." I kiss her forehead. "You and Bella were worth the wait."

"The wait for what?" she asks.

"My family. My real family. If it's only ever the three of us,"

"And Mouse," she interrupts.

"And Mouse," I add with a smile. "Then I'll be the happiest man in the world."

"I know you've already made me the happiest woman in the world."

"Ugh, y'all are sickening," comes a man's voice from the door.

"Romeo," I say. "What the hell, man, my wife's tit is out."

"She's breastfeeding," Romeo says with a shrug.

"I don't mind," Daisy says. "Baby girl's head covers all your favorite parts," she whispers to me.

Then all the guys are piling into the room, and the wives too. Those who have them. We've made quite the home here in Saddle Creek. My Ranger unit only had one soldier claiming this town as their own when we all met. But now we all live here, all claim this little piece of Texas heaven as our home.

"I think she's done," Daisy says.

"Everyone turn around and face the other direction, "I say.

Daisy laughs as they all follow my instructions.

She tucks herself back into her gown and hands my daughter to me. My daughter.

"She needs to be burped, then y'all can meet her and take all your pictures," I tell our friends. "You're going to want pictures because she's the most beautiful little girl in the entire world." After getting a little burp, I hand Bella off to her Aunt Temple.

I kiss my wife's head. "Only fitting since you're the most beautiful woman in the world."

***

I hope you loved Beau and Daisy's story. Please consider **leaving me a review**.

Read the other books in the Dog Tags series:

Jack of Hearts

Fools Rush Flynn

Quid Pro Beau

Love 'em or Liam

Happily Evan After

Ready, Willing and Abel

Romero and Juliette

Grab **Redeem My Heart** if you want to see where Great Dane's Dog Sanctuary started.

Keep scrolling for another hot military man story, **Curves and Cradles**

thank you for reading!

Join my newsletter for bonus epilogues, deleted scenes and a FREE BOOK.

join me!

COME JOIN my **VIP Reader Group on Facebook** where I do sneak peeks, answer questions and keep you up to date with everyone going on in Kat Baxter land.

excerpt from curves and cradles

Kevin

. . .

I TAKE a swig of my beer and look at the brunette a few stools over.

We've been exchanging glances for the last twenty minutes. She tripped when she first entered the bar, caught me watching, and flashed me an adorably goofy grin that went straight to my dick.

Awkward or not, the girl is hot. Petite and curvy in all the right places, like a pinup girl you find leaning against a muscle car.

Between her occasional gaze and smile, she divides her time between staring at her phone and watching the door. She's clearly waiting for someone.

My phone buzzes, and I glance down.

Cade: Met w/funeral dir.
Sucked. See you tomorrow.

Damn. I came to Texas for Lieutenant Cade Wilson from SEAL Team Seven. We've been best friends since I was in BUD/S training. When it came down to it, there was no question about me coming to help my friend bury his mother. No one should do that alone. I might not know what it's like to have a family in the traditional sense of the word, but his team is all the family I need. And this—using my weekend leave to support Cade—is what I'd do for any of my brothers.

I know how to support my team in the field. I know I'm prepared to take a bullet for any and all of them. What I don't know is how to support someone through the loss of a loved one. I've never had anyone, and therefore I've never lost anyone. It keeps my life tidy, at least in the emotional sense.

When I look up from my phone, the cute girl I've been eyeing has disappeared. Evidently, whomever she was waiting for finally arrived. Damn. I was hoping for some company tonight. It's been too long since I got laid, and her heart-shaped ass and nice rack were just what I needed.

I spin on my barstool to face the darkened room behind me. There are no neon signs advertising the variety of beers. Nor are there any pool tables. This isn't the type of bar I usually pick. Hell, I don't even know what kind of music is pumping from the speakers, but it's across the street from the hotel, so it's convenient. I didn't bother to change into nicer clothes, and I'm still wearing the jeans and T-shirt I traveled in. My hand goes to my neck to ensure my dog tags are still tucked inside my shirt.

A new group enters the bar and shuffles up to order drinks. All the guys are wearing skinny jeans and beanies—bunch of damned hipsters.

I should've known this was a hipster bar when it took the bartender fifteen minutes to list all the craft beers. Maybe I should head back to my hotel and order room service. I take another swallow of my Shiner and set the bottle on the bar behind me.

Then sexy-awkward girl steps out of the bathroom, and her eyes move to the new group of customers. Something in her features wilts, and she bites her lip. She's expressive. Yeah, she's definitely working for me.

As if I've called to her, her attention slides to me. Determination sets her features, and she starts toward me. There's nothing inherently sexy in her no-nonsense walk, nor her clothes—basic jeans and a shirt with black Converse tennis shoes—still, there's something about her that I can't tear my eyes from.

Hell, yeah, baby.

Uncertainty flickers across her face once she reaches me.

I wait for her to speak.

She glances at the new group at the bar, positions herself between my legs, and kisses me as if her life depends on it.

Her full tits press into my chest, and I lower my hands to her hips, gripping her tightly, holding her to me. After a moment of shock, I tilt my head and take control of the kiss, sliding my tongue against hers. We taste and tease one another. She moans into my mouth, and my cock hardens behind my zipper. I groan, frustrated that we're in a bar and she's wearing clothes.

She leans back and gives me a shy smile, fingering the chain around my neck. "I'm hoping that your ball chain and buzz cut mean you're not a terrible person." Her voice is lower than I expected, sultry and husky and sexy as fuck. "I mean, people who join the army can't be total creepers, right?" she continues. "Anyway, would you please go along with this, and I'll explain later?"

"Navy," I correct.

Her head tilts. "What?"

"You said army. I'm Navy."

Her mouth opens, but she says nothing.

"Jane? Is that you?"

One of the hipsters sidles up beside us. He pushes his dark-rimmed glasses up his nose. Damn tool is even wearing a plaid shirt, half tucked into his skinny jeans. A tall, thin blonde stands next to him, gripping his arm.

I resist the urge to roll my eyes. Instead, I pull her—Jane—closer so she's between my thighs, leaning against my chest. I wrap an arm around her waist and let the other rest on her incredible breasts.

"Uh, hey, Blake," she says. "I didn't realize you were back in town."

The perky blonde next to him holds up her hand and gives a little jump. "We're engaged!"

Blake grabs his fiancée's hand and holds it close to his side. "You look great, Jane." Then his gaze flickers to me. "So, what's going on with you two?"

Ah, so this must be an ex of hers, and she's using me to make him jealous. Not my preferred scenario, but if it keeps Jane in my arms, I'll take it.

"Kevin," I say to introduce myself, then reach around Jane to grab the tool's hand. "Janie and I are together." I lower my feet from the barstool rungs to the floor and press against her backside.

"Janie?" Blake asks. "I thought you hated being called anything but Jane." He frowns as he pushes up his dark-rimmed glasses again.

"I don't mind so much when Kevin says it."

I lean forward and lower my chin to her shoulder. "Super awesome to meet you."

Jane's stomach clenches beneath my arm as she suppresses a laugh.

Blake frowns and looks back at Jane. "Sure. Well, it was great seeing you, *Jane.*" He emphasizes her name. "Maybe we can catch up sometime."

His fiancée looks annoyed by that thought, but he puts his hand on her lower back and leads her away. The three couples settle into a booth in the back corner.

Jane spins and braces her hands on my thighs to keep herself from falling over. "Thank you."

"Well, it was the least I could do after that

kiss." I smile at her. "I take it you and Blake, the hipster, have history?"

"Yes. We dated through high school and on and off through the first part of college." Her eyes search my face. They're blue, but sorta gray, too—an unusual shade. And there's that adorable grin again. "God, you're super hot." Her mouth drops open, and her eyes widen. "I can't believe I just said that. Also can't believe I jumped on you like that. I'm sorry."

"You think I'm super hot?"

She rolls her eyes. "Don't pretend to be modest. No one looks like you and doesn't realize he looks like a sex god."

My brows rise. "A sex god, huh?"

She leans forward, bracing her forehead on my chest.

"You smell good," I murmur.

"Thanks." She smiles. "My friend was supposed to meet me here, but a work thing came up, and she couldn't make it."

I'm pleased she was meeting a girlfriend rather than another guy.

"I'm hoping you can do me one more favor...can we walk out of here like we're going home together? Then I promise I'll totally leave you alone."

I shake my head. "That is unacceptable."

"What?"

"I'll walk out with you, but now that I know you think I'm a sex god, I'm not quite ready to let you go. Know anywhere around here we can get a good burger?"

Her face splits into a toothy grin. "I sure do."

I drape an arm over her shoulder. "Then lead the way, babe, because I'm starving."

Grab your copy of **Curves and Cradles**

about the author

USA Today Bestselling Author, Kat Baxter writes fast-paced, sweet & STEAMY romantic comedies. Readers have dubbed her "The Queen of Adorkable." and her books "laugh-out-loud funny," and "hot enough to melt your kindle." She lives in Texas with her family and a menagerie of animals. Kat is the pseudonym for a bestselling historical romance author.

What readers have said about Kat's books:

"Kat Baxter is my catnip!" ~ Goodreads review

"Whenever I need my sexy nerdy dirty talking romance fix, I know Kat Baxter has my back!" ~Goodreads review

"How does Kat Baxter make me fall in love with her characters in just 12 short chapters? It's coz she's a freaken magic weaver with her words!!" ~ Amazon review

"You'll instantly fall in love." ~Goodreads review

"Swoon. I could not get enough of this story and fell in love with both these characters!" ~Amazon review

"... the chemistry between them is instant and off the charts!" ~Amazon review

"... original, hot, and a hoot!" ~Amazon review

"DAMN it's hot." ~Amazon review

"... sweetness, heat and humor. By the time the story was over, my cheeks hurt from smiling so hard." ~Amazon review

"Such a very sweet and spicy story!" ~ Goodreads

"The connection between the characters felt real, and I liked the author's writing style." ~ Goodreads

Made in the USA
Coppell, TX
20 January 2026

68886356R00085